Out +
About

KU-453-085

Tony Bradman has written many books for children o   s,
and has been published all over the world. He has also edited
a large number of highly successful anthologies of short stories and
poems, including *Give me Shelter* and *Under the Weather*
for Frances Lincoln. His other books for Frances Lincoln are
This Little Baby, Look Out He's Behind You and *Has Anyone Seen Jack?*
Tony lives in Beckenham, Kent.

Eileen Browne worked as a school teacher and youth worker
before becoming an author and illustrator. Her best known books are
Handa's Surprise, Handa's Hen and *No Problem*. *Handa's Surprise*
and *No Problem* were both shortlisted for awards.
Eileen lives in Wiltshire.

Tony and Eileen have also worked together on *Through my Window*
and *Wait and See*, both published by Frances Lincoln.

For Stella, Toni and Biko – E.B.

For Anna – T.B.

Text copyright © Tony Bradman and Eileen Browne 1990
Illustrations copyright © Eileen Browne 1990

First published in Great Britain in 1990 by Methuen Children's Books Ltd

This edition published in 2011 by Frances Lincoln Children's Books,
4 Torriano Mews, Torriano Avenue, London NW5 2RZ
www.franceslincoln.com

A catalogue record for this book is available from the British Library.

ISBN 978-1-84780-180-7

Printed in Shenzhen, Guangdong, China by C&C Offset Printing Co., Ltd. in November 2010

1 3 5 7 9 8 6 4 2

IN A MINUTE

Tony Bradman and Eileen Browne

F

FRANCES LINCOLN
CHILDREN'S BOOKS

"I'm ready!" said Jo.
She was going to the park
with her mum and dad.

Best of all, she was going to the playground
with its swings, see-saw and slide.
Sita and her dog, Patch, were coming too.

"Can we go now?" asked Jo.
But Mum and Dad were very slow.
"We'll be with you in a minute," they said.

Soon Mum and Dad were ready.
They went next door for Sita.

"Come in," called Sita's mum.

She was putting something in a bag.

Sita was looking for Patch's lead.
"Be with you in a minute," she said.

Now Sita was ready.

They set off for the bus stop.
But on the way, Dad met one of his friends.

They stopped to chat.
"Dad!" said Jo. "We'll miss the bus!"
"I'll be with you in a minute," said Dad.
He kept on talking.

They missed the bus.

"Oh well," said Mum.
"There will be another one along . . ."
"In a minute!" said Jo.
But they had to wait for ages.

At last, they arrived
at the park.

They were just going in
when Mum met one of *her* friends.

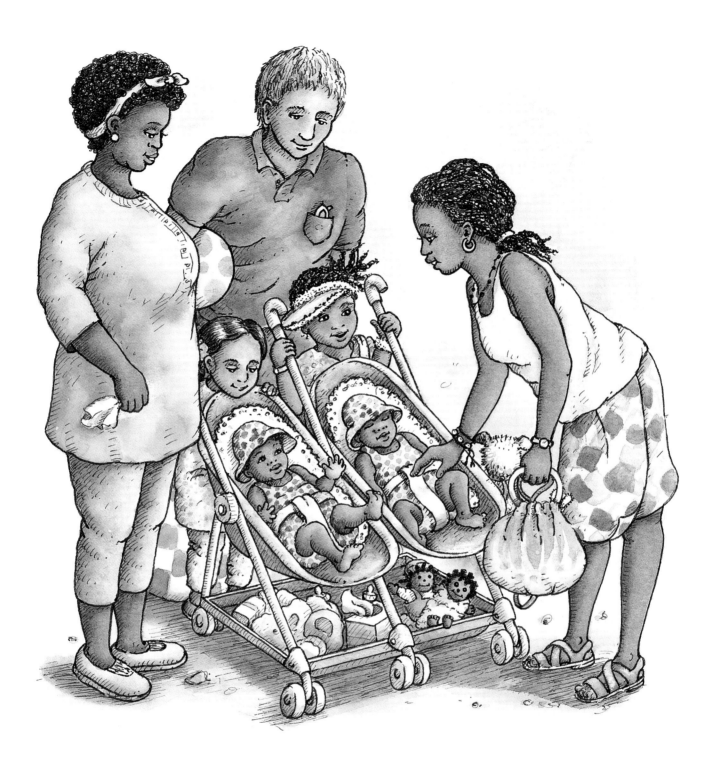

So they stopped for another chat,
and to look in the buggy.
"Mum, can we go in now?" asked Jo.
"In a minute, Jo," said her mum.

They went into the park.
"This way to the playground!"
said Jo and Sita.

But Mum and Dad stopped to listen
to a woman making a speech.

Jo tugged her dad's arm.
"We'll be with you in a minute," said Dad.

They walked on and came to the duckpond.
Jo could see the playground
in the distance.

"Let's feed the ducks," said Mum.

Jo wanted to run on.
"Stay with us, Jo," said Mum.
"We'll be with you in a minute."

They left the duckpond
and walked towards the playground.

But then a carnival procession came by
and they stopped to listen to
the steel band.

"We'll never get to the playground," said Jo.
"Yes we will," said Dad.
"We'll be there in a minute."

At last they were at the playground!
Jo and Sita ran in through the gate.
But something terrible had happened.

The swings were tied in knots.
The see-saw was broken
and the slide had chains round it.

"It's not fair," cried Jo.

Suddenly Patch ran off.
"Quick, after her!" shouted Mum.
Jo and Sita chased Patch round the corner.
What do you think they found?

A fantastic new playground!

"Wow!" said Jo.
"Brilliant!" said Sita.
There were four bright red swings,

a stripy see-saw
and a great big elephant slide.

Jo and Sita swung . . .

and bounced . . .

and slid . . .
until they were tired.

Then they all sat in the shade
and had a picnic.

"Come on, you two," said Mum and Dad.
"It's time to go home."
Can you guess what Jo and Sita said?

That's right!
"We'll be with you . . . IN A MINUTE!"

MORE PAPERBACKS FROM FRANCES LINCOLN CHILDREN'S BOOKS

Through My Window
Tony Bradman and Eileen Browne

When Jo has to stay in bed for the day, her dad
looks after her and her mum promises to bring her
a special surprise present home from work.
While Jo waits, she looks out of her window at all
the goings-on in the street, and gets more and more
excited about what her mum's special surprise will be. . .

Wait and See
Tony Bradman and Eileen Browne

It's Saturday, and Jo has some money to spend.
So she and her mum go shopping, while Dad stays
at home to make lunch for them all.
But what should she spend her money on?
And what will they do when Patch the dog ruins
their lunch plans?
She'll have to wait and see.

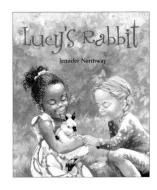

Lucy's Rabbit
A Lucy and Alice story
Jennifer Northway

Lucy is busy making decorations for her mum's birthday
with the help of her cousin Alice. When they discover
a rabbit eating Dad's pansies they think it is a great idea
for a surprise present. But keeping the rabbit out of
trouble for long enough to give her to Mum is harder
than they expect.